A KENYA CHRISTMAS

by
Tony
Johnston

illustrated by
Leonard
Jenkins

Holiday House / *New York*

With special thanks to Castro Wesamba,
Second Secretary of the Kenya Mission
to the United Nations, for his help.

Library of Congress Cataloging-in-Publication Data

Johnston, Tony, 1942–
A Kenya Christmas / by Tony Johnston; illustrated by Leonard Jenkins.—1st ed.
p. cm.
Summary: Ten-year-old Juma and his aunt Aida plan to surprise his Kenyan village
with an appearance by Father Christmas and find that they themselves are surprised.

ISBN 0-8234-1623-2 (hardcover)
[1. Christmas—Fiction. 2. Santa Claus—Fiction. 3. Kenya—Fiction.
4. Aunts—Fiction.] I. Jenkins, Leonard, ill. II. Title.
PZ7.J6478 Ke 2003
[E]—dc21
2002192197

For Sophia, Rishi, and Saurabh,
"They're from Nairobi and
they are the best . . . ."
T. J.

For Marline and Ujijji Martin,
my friends who posed for this book
L. L. J.

Every December my rich aunt Aida came to visit us from Nairobi. I remember one Christmas very well, the year that I was ten.

One day, like a dust devil, Aunt Aida swirled up the path. Beside her romped her pet cheetahs, Pomp and Circumstance.

Thump. She dropped her bags down on our *banda* floor.

"*Jambo!*" she cried. "I am here!"

Aunt Aida wasted no time. First she hugged us so hard, if we'd been kola nuts we'd surely have cracked. Then she asked me, "Juma, my sweet, what is your number-one Christmas wish?"

I always wished for the same thing.

"To see Father Christmas," I said.

We children received small gifts—oranges, carved dolls, sometimes shoes. But not even Father Christmas's helper had ever come here, our village was so far.

"A fine wish," my auntie told me, as she did each year. "I shall see what I can do."

The way her eyes sparkled, I knew she had done something already.

That night, when everyone else was sleeping, I heard a soft *hssst! hssst!*—like water sizzling in the fire. I sat up and saw Aunt Aida and the cheetahs creeping close. Their eyes glowed like coals.

"Look, Juma," she whispered with excitement. Then she opened a large bundle and lifted out a splendid blanket of red.

I looked again. It was a Father Christmas suit!

"Find someone to wear this on Christmas Eve," she said, "and the whole village will have your wish."

The days were one long secret, as we planned this Christmas surprise. Our whispers filled the air like wind in the tall grass.

It was easy to find a Father Christmas. Ole Tunai, the chicken man, had always dreamed of such a job. Though tall and thin, he promised me that for the occasion he would make himself properly plump.

Aunt Aida took charge of the gifts. Shopping was her specialty.

"What about a sleigh?" I asked her.

"A problem," she said thoughtfully. "Sleighs do not grow here like bananas on trees."

So instead of a sleigh, Aunt Aida ordered an elephant for Father Christmas to ride.

"But Tembo will not carry people," the elephant owner insisted. "He cannot be tamed."

But Aunt Aida insisted more. With Pomp and Circumstance at her side, the man did not refuse.

"What about snow?" Aunt Aida asked me. From the many holiday cards she'd seen on her travels, she knew this to be a necessity.

"A problem," I said.

My best friend, Nampaso, and I collected chicken feathers in grain sacks. Though most of the feathers were speckled or brown, they would be our snow.

The days crept slowly by, like they do when we wait for the rain.
But at long last Christmas Eve came.

All the villagers knew by now that something would happen this night.
Like magic, the people gathered together. They ate *mandazis* and *chapatis*
and sang Christmas songs while awaiting the wonderful thing.

Suddenly, there came a swish of leaves. From out of the bush a great elephant
slowly strode, like a great ship on the sea. High up on top Father Christmas rode.

A hush fell over everything. Even the animals slowed. For a moment we were all part of a secret, deep and old.

Then the people cheered with delight. The spell was broken.

I hardly recognized Ole Tunai in his costume, red as a pomegranate and grand. Nampaso and I danced beside Tembo the elephant, tossing chicken-feather snow all about.

Everyone was excited. The children jumped like young locusts. The old people jumped like old locusts. Soon Tembo stooped and knelt, and Father Christmas slid down.

The cheetahs were so excited, they chased him up a tree!

"Stop that, you naughty boys!" Aunt Aida cried, shooing them off.

Father Christmas smiled, springing to the ground—springing as much as he could, for one so fat. He sipped hot *chai*, then gave out gifts—toy cars, *kangas*, bicycles, too! When the toys were gone, he nimbly climbed up on Tembo and rode back into the bush.

"*Kwaheri!*" everyone called.

Some people peeked for one last glimpse at the spot where he had gone. But he had vanished—like smoke.

So, chattering, the villagers walked away. Slowly, like melting snow. Congratulating ourselves loudly over our success, Aunt Aida and Nampaso and I frolicked all the way home.

Soon, Ole Tunai shuffled into our *banda*, hoisting his pillow belly. We rushed to praise his fine work. But he was nearly in tears.

"I am sorry," he said sadly again and again.

"But why?"

"Tembo behaved most badly. He would not allow me to ride," he wailed. "I have failed everyone."

We stared at one another. Then outside, from high above, I heard a sound.
A shout. "HAPPY CHRISTMAS!" We rushed out and saw a great elephant climbing
the starlit sky. Seated on top, Father Christmas waved down.
For a long time we stood in silence, as stiff as baobab trees.

"You naughty, *naughty* boys for chasing that fine fat man!"
my auntie scolded the cheetahs, horrified.
"Our plan worked," I said.
Then we laughed. And we cried.

Now I am old. Each December my grandchildren
gather about me, jumping like young locusts.
  "A story, *Baba*! A story!" they plead.
  "Which one?" I tease.
  "The story, *Baba*, of when you were a boy."
  So I begin. "I remember one Christmas very well.
The year that I was ten."

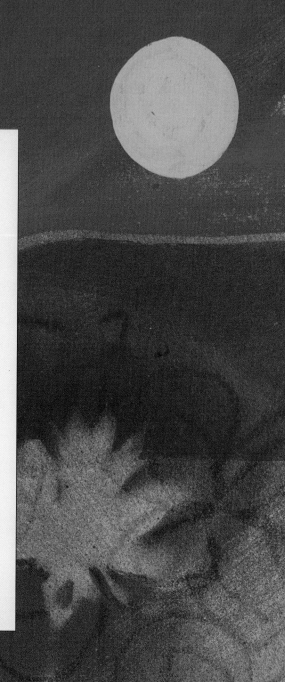

Glossary

baba—grandfather

banda—hut

baobab—a kind of tree

bush—the wilderness

chai—tea

chapati—African bread

jambo—hello

kanga—cloth sarong

Kenya—an African country

kola—a type of nut

kwaheri—good-bye

mandazi—African doughnut

Nairobi—capital of Kenya

tembo—elephant tusk